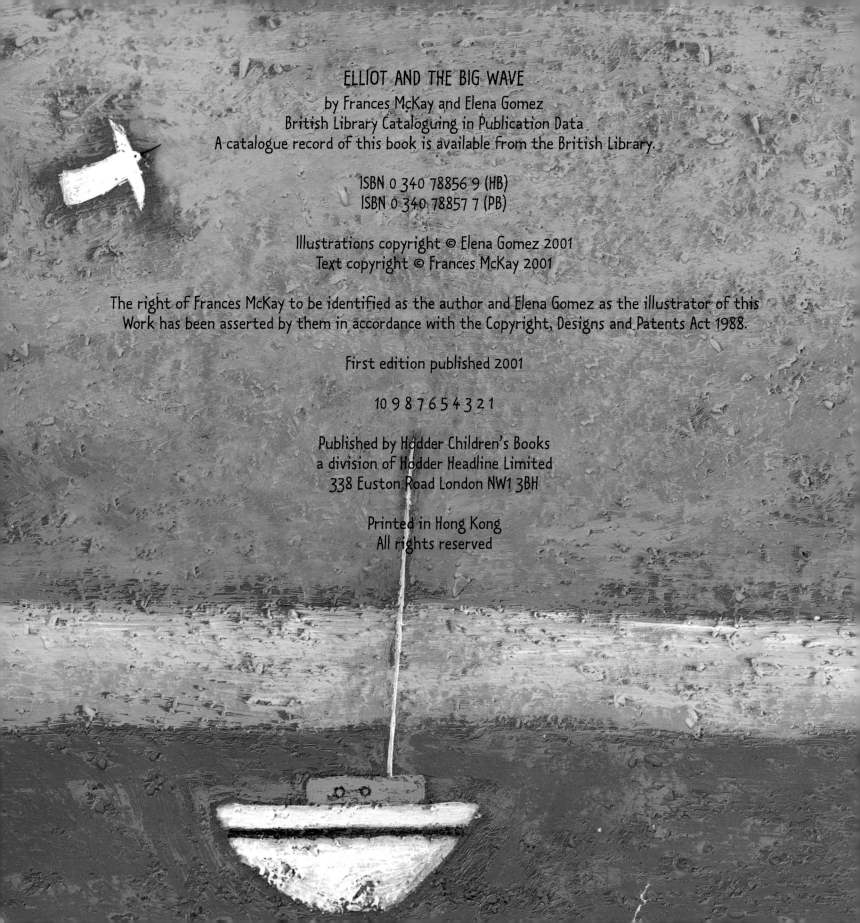

ELLIOT AND THE BIG WAVE
by Frances McKay and Elena Gomez
British Library Cataloguing in Publication Data
A catalogue record of this book is available from the British Library.

ISBN 0 340 78856 9 (HB)
ISBN 0 340 78857 7 (PB)

Illustrations copyright © Elena Gomez 2001
Text copyright © Frances McKay 2001

First edition published 2001

10 9 8 7 6 5 4 3 2 1

Published by Hodder Children's Books
a division of Hodder Headline Limited
338 Euston Road London NW1 3BH

Printed in Hong Kong

Elliot and the Big Wave

Frances McKay and Elena Gomez

Hodder Children's Books

A division of Hodder Headline Limited

Elliot lived with Bernard in
the old lighthouse on the harbour
wall. He loved the smell of the
sea and chasing the seagulls.

One day, the sun was shining and the wind was blowing.
'What a lovely day to go fishing,' said Bernard.
Fish! thought Elliot. My favourite.

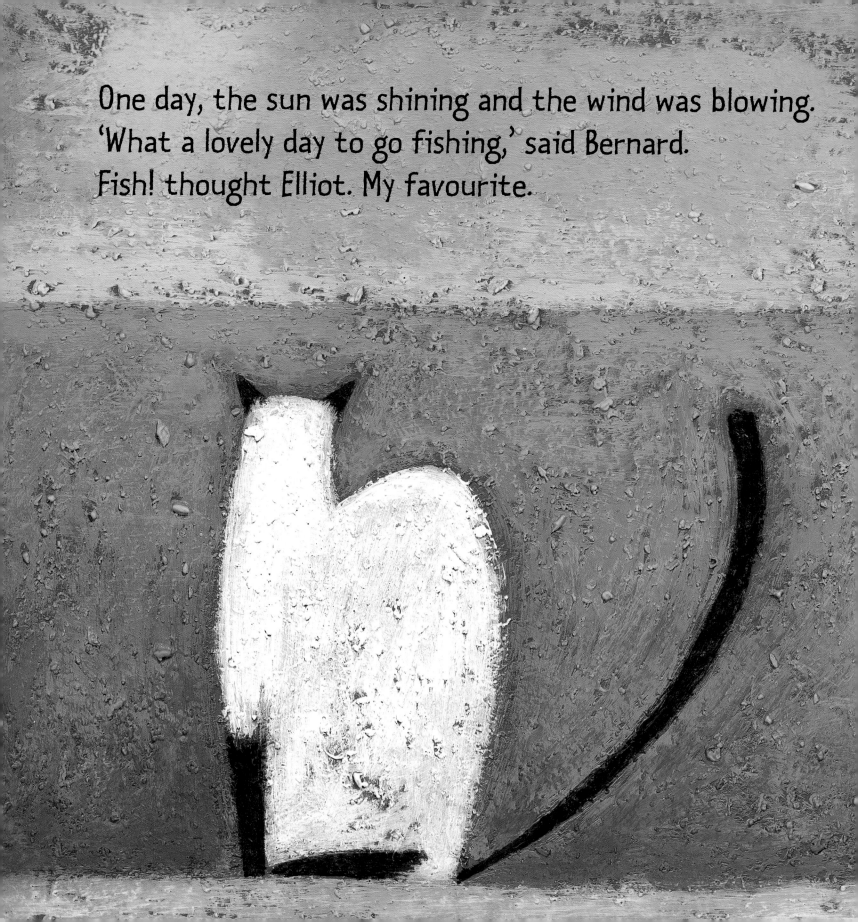

I wonder if I can do fishing? thought Elliot.
Bother. I can almost reach . . . but not quite.

Perhaps I'll go fishing with Bernard.
He won't even know I'm there.

Out at sea there were lots of fish.
Lots of fish that didn't want to be caught.
Bother, bother. I still can't reach,
thought Elliot. Then . . .

Boom! A big wave hit the boat.

Oh no! thought Elliot. Maybe this wasn't such a good idea after all.

Down went Elliot and down went the bucket and down went the mop. Bother, bother, bother, thought Elliot. I still can't reach the fish! But what is that trying to reach me?

Suddenly the bucket floated past. Elliot jumped in. That's a bit of luck, he thought.

Then another huge wave caught the bucket.
Oh no, thought Elliot, this is really not my day.
But the wave carried the bucket back to shore . . .

. . . and tipped him out onto the beach. Elliot decided that was quite enough fishing for one day. He ran along the beach, up the steps to the harbour wall, and raced all the way home.

Elliot sat shivering and waited
for Bernard to come home.
'Oh, Elliot, you're soaking!
Has it been raining? You should have come
fishing with me. It's been a perfect day.'
Purrfect for you, thought Elliot, grumpily.

That evening, there was
one fish Elliot could reach.

Well, maybe it hasn't been such a bad day
after all, smiled Elliot. And at least I tried,
he thought happily, at least I tried and . . .

But Elliot was already asleep.

For

Mark Elliot

EG

Josh and Imogen

FM